THE SILVER NUTMEG

BY THE SAME AUTHOR

THE SILVER NUTMEG

THE STORY OF ANNA LAVINIA AND TOBY

by

PALMER BROWN

with pictures by the author

THE NEW YORK REVIEW
CHILDREN'S COLLECTION
New York

THIS IS A NEW YORK REVIEW BOOK
PUBLISHED BY THE NEW YORK REVIEW OF BOOKS
435 Hudson Street, New York, NY 10014
www.nyrb.com

Library of Congress Cataloging-in-Publication Data
Brown, Palmer.
The silver nutmeg / by Palmer Brown ; illustrations by Palmer
Brown.
p. cm. — (New York Review books children's collection)
Companion to: Beyond the pawpaw trees.
Summary: One dull, dry day Anna Livinia meets Toby, who invites
her into the wondrous world on the other side of Dew Pond, where
she encounters an uncanny fortuneteller, experiences the fun of no
gravity, and hears Aunt Cornelia's tale of her beloved who disap-
peared into Anna's world.
ISBN 978-1-59017-500-2 (alk. paper)
[1. Fantasy.] I. Title.
PZ7.B816647Si 2012
[Fic]—dc23
                                                2011029307

ISBN 978-1-59017-500-2
Cover design by Louise Fili Ltd.
Printed in the United States on acid-free paper.
1 3 5 7 9 10 8 6 4 2

CONTENTS

CHAPTER I

A NEW POINT OF VIEW

ATE SUMMER had never been so hot and dry. In the back yard Anna Lavinia leaned against the side of the well, looking into its darkness. Though it was still early in the day, she felt the stones beneath her fingers already warm with sunlight.

"Ho!" she shouted down the well.

"Pouf," the echo came back faintly.

"Ho! Ho!" she called again.

"Pouf-ouf," the answer came, like a cork pulled from an empty jug.

It was no good. The well was still dry, and the echo would not answer clearly. When water filled the well, it echoed back the slightest whisper. Now it had been dry for weeks. Anna Lavinia knew that when her mother called to her soon for more water, she would have to take her pail beyond the garden wall to the spring that ran under the bridge on the road to the village.

Because it was so very dry, the pawpaws had been dropping unripe from the pawpaw trees that ringed the yard, and Anna Lavinia's

mother, who hated to see anything go to waste, had been putting up jar after jar of green pawpaw preserves. The whole house smelled of spices and vinegar and minced onions, and though the smell was pleasant for a little while, eventually it made the eyes

water. These days Anna Lavinia kept out of the house as much as possible. She knew that if her father had been home, instead of away on one of his trips, her mother would never have bothered with the green pawpaw preserves. Her father had too sensitive a nose. But nothing seemed to go quite right when he was away.

Anna Lavinia bent down to look in on her pet hedgehog, which slept in the fern-covered hollow near the well, and she sang to it two lines from her favorite book, *Songs from Nowhere:*

Good morning, Mr. Brimming-plate,
Have breakfast with me, do!

Any other time the hedgehog would have opened one eye to wink at her, but lately it had been grumpy because its favorite thistles had grown parched and tough. Today it refused to twitch a quill. So Anna Lavinia left the hedgehog, singing the rest of the verse to herself:

Ah! thank you, Mrs. Ask-too-late,
I'll not break fast with you:
I eat when dawn's as pink as prawns,
Now the sun is boiling through.

Halfway across the withered lawn Anna Lavinia met her ginger cat, Strawberry, washing his whiskers after his breakfast cream. To him she sang the next lines:

Good day, dear Mr. Brimming-plate,
Have luncheon with me, do!

Strawberry did not bother to look up at her, but waved his tail and trotted off towards the garden gate. Anna Lavinia knew he would wriggle underneath it and then find his usual cool spot beside the spring. Hot weather made him want to be alone. So she sang the rest of that verse to herself:

Ah! thank you, Mrs. Ask-too-late,
I cannot lunch with you:
I lunch at one in the lobster sun,
    Now the clock is clapping two.

Near the house Anna Lavinia stopped beside the nasturtium bed to look at the thobby, a stubby-tailed polka-dotted lizard which had been a present to her once. She sang:

> Good evening, Mr. Brimming-plate,
> Have dinner with me, do!

The thobby, who was unhappy because the nasturtiums gave so little of his favorite honey-dew these dry days, went right on burrowing a damp hole in the center of the flower bed. Walking on, Anna Lavinia sang to herself again:

> Ah! thank you, Mrs. Ask-too-late,
> I cannot dine with you:
> I dine when the sun is a bitten bun,
> Now the fish-scale moon is new.

At the back stoop Anna Lavinia took off her shoes. There on a lattice hung with cinnamon vine perched her red and purple parrot, driven from its kitchen cage by the onion smell. Anna Lavinia looked up at the parrot and sang:

> Have tea, then, Mr. Brimming-plate,
> You name the hour, please, do!

Now, of all her pets, the parrot alone could really have answered, if it had wanted to. But it had been stubbornly silent for days. Instead of even glancing down at Anna Lavinia, it solemnly cracked a sunflower seed, letting the shell plop to the back stoop. Again she had to sing just to herself:

> No! thank you, Mrs. Ask-too-late,
> I'll not take tea with you:
> Your tea, I'm told, is oyster-cold,
> And I must have biscuits too.

"Good-bye, then, Mr. Brimming-plate,"

Anna Lavinia said, and she sat down on the stoop and began to hammer at a peach stone with one of her shoes to get the nut-like kernel out. Yet, tap as she might, the stone would not break.

That was a bad sign, she felt. It made her wonder whether the day would be good for anything at all. Sometimes a very little thing, like whether a peach stone would crack or not, seemed to make all the difference. Her father told her once that every day was a sort of adventure, and she believed it. But she also knew that some days were better than others.

The very best of all were those wonderful days when the sky was lavender blue.

It was a lavender blue day that had brought her the hedgehog from the other side of the garden wall where buttercups bloomed pink. It was a lavender blue day that had taken her and Strawberry on their only trip beyond the wall, and from that trip they had come home bringing the parrot and the thobby. If only the sky could show some hint of lavender, something special might take place today.

Still the peach stone refused to crack, and at last Anna Lavinia cast it aside and looked out across the lawn to the jagged opening in the garden wall. Far in the distance she saw Dew Pond Hill, with its green crown of old oaks caught in a smoky net of blue haze. The waves of heat made it twist and ripple like a reflection on windblown water.

The unfinished break in the garden wall was a part of her father's new plan to broaden the horizon for her. "It is shameful," he had said to her mother one day, "for Anna Lavinia to be cooped up. How can you expect the girl to grow up with a point of view, if she has none?"

Anna Lavinia secretly felt that she had points of view on many things, but she had been thrilled with her father's decision to help her find a new one. For a whole week she and her father had tramped around the outside of the rosy brick wall, figuring out just the right place to open it.

The choice finally went to Dew Pond Hill. As hills went, it was on the small side, but that did not make it unimportant. "After all," her father had said, "there are dozens of mountains in the world, but very few hills with dew ponds on top." Anna Lavinia was delighted at that. Her point of view would be something extra-special.

For another whole week they were busy tearing down part of the wall. Standing on a ladder, her father would hand each brick to her as he pried it loose. She would then set the brick in place on the lawn to make a garden walk to the back stoop. Two bricks this way and two bricks that way, with spaces between to plant wild thyme.

But the hole was only half finished, and with her father away it did not seem as though it would ever be done. By standing on three bricks set against the wall Anna Lavinia could just climb over what was left, but it was not yet a practical hole. To fetch water from the spring she still used the gate. Her mother would give her the key and, hole or no hole, she had to lock the gate each time she came or went. "It keeps the lock from rusting," her mother explained.

Just now, as her mother stuck her head out the back door for a moment to get the onion tears out of her eyes, she tossed the key to Anna Lavinia. "More water soon, dear," she said. "I'm about ready to start a new batch of the green pawpaw preserves."

The screen door slammed shut. A spotted dragonfly rested on one of the leaves of the cinnamon vine and then darted away. Far off the haze on Dew Pond Hill simmered, now with just a tinge of lavender. Across a field at the foot of the hill three men were walking with shovels slanted across their shoulders.

From the kitchen her mother called again, "And try not to be all morning. I have that feeling someone will be coming."

Anna Lavinia jumped to her feet. Her mother was never wrong about such feelings. "Do you think it is Father coming home?" she cried.

"No, that's a different feeling," her mother answered.

Anna Lavinia stooped to pick up her pail, and then she put it down. Grabbing a shoe, she thumped it against the peach stone as hard as she could. It split neatly, and she was sure that it was a good sign. Something was going to happen after all. She popped the kernel in her mouth and threw the pieces of shell over her left shoulder. Then she snatched her pail again and ran for the gate.

CHAPTER 2

PAGES IN AN OLD BOOK

THE SPRING shimmered in the sun. Welling up from a small grotto over-hung with ferns, the water tumbled between sloping banks, catching sunlight at every ripple. At one time long ago someone had built a stone spring-house over the opening, but like quicksilver the water had slithered between the stones. Bit by bit the mortar

had washed away and the stones had fallen,
leaving only part of a low wall, tufted with
rock flowers and furred with moss. It was at
the foot of this wall that Strawberry spent the
hot days. With his front paws curled against
his chest and his eyes three-quarters shut he
watched the silver minnows that stood
motionless in the current.

Several of the fallen rocks formed stepping-stones across the stream, and Anna Lavinia knelt on one of these to fill her pail. She
tried to scoop a pail of minnows, but every
time they fled between the rocks and hid
themselves in the islands of blue water-hya-
cinths floating in the quiet shallows. Deep in
the hollow where the water arose, Anna
Lavinia saw the white throats and golden
eyes of the frogs that sat upon a ledge of wet

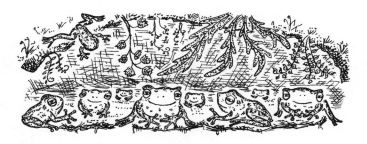

rock. When she tried to wade towards them, however, the water grew deeper and colder with each step. Shivering a little, she filled her pail and sat on the bank to dry her feet in the sun. Bits of a dry stick which she tossed into the current swirled downstream, and she watched them disappear beneath the bridge, and she wondered where they would put in to shore.

The sound of her mother's voice calling to her from the gate interrupted her wondering, and Anna Lavinia climbed the embankment to the road. When she reached the top, she saw why her mother was calling, and she began to run, sloshing the water in the pail. Her mother stood inside the garden gate, rattling it impatiently. On the other side, unable to get in because Anna Lavinia had the key, stood Anna Lavinia's Uncle Jeffrey, a knapsack over his shoulder, and his bald head pink in the sun.

"Is the spring running dry too, that you were so long?" her mother asked, as Anna Lavinia turned the key in the lock.

"I would have come through that hole in the wall I see over there," her Uncle Jeffrey said, tweaking Anna Lavinia's ear as he always did when he came to visit, "but I'm not so nimble as I used to be."

He took the pail from her, and she ran on ahead to hold open the kitchen door. Looking back at him crossing the lawn with her mother, Anna Lavinia thought he seemed as nimble as ever. Small and wiry, he was just a bit bowlegged, so that he seemed to skip as he walked, as though he were dancing. He wore the same old patched tweed suit that he always wore when he dropped in once or twice a year, and into the buttonhole of his jacket he had thrust one of the last pink buttercups of the season. As he danced across the lawn, the buttercup bobbed on its stem.

Spry though her Uncle Jeffrey was, Anna Lavinia knew he was very old—much older than her father. He was not really Anna Lavinia's uncle at all, but a sort of great uncle, twice removed. On his last visit Anna Lavinia had asked him where he was twice removed from, and why. It was sometimes hard to ask him a question, because he was a little deaf, though Anna Lavinia's mother said he was deaf only if it suited him to be.

When Anna Lavinia had finally made him understand her question, he had laughed in his high-pitched way, and he had answered that it was something of a secret and too long a story anyway. Later her mother told her that she should think twice before asking foolish questions. But when Anna Lavinia wanted to know how thinking twice about it could help if you still wanted to learn the answer, her mother just shook her head.

Today, sitting at the kitchen table, Anna Lavinia was careful to be silent as the sun-parched garden, while her mother leaned over the stove toasting cheese sandwiches for lunch. Uncle Jeffrey skipped about the room to lift the lids of the kettles and inspect the heaps of sliced green pawpaws and minced onions and celery, and he sniffed at all the piles of spices measured out for the next batch of preserves. Anna Lavinia watched him go to the spice cabinet and pull out each drawer to see which ones were empty. Then, as he did on each visit, he set all the empty drawers in a row on the kitchen table. From his knapsack he unpacked a great number of little green glass bottles and painted tin boxes.

As he filled the empty drawers, weighing out the spices with brass scales, he sang his song of the spices. The words were different on each visit, for they mentioned only what was needed that day. Today the words ran:

Here's cinnamon from far Ceylon,
    From Mexico vanilla,
Cloves from groves of Zanzibar,
    Coconut from Manila.

Here's ginger in Jamaica grown,
    Mace from the Spanish Main,
Nutmeg from sands by Javan strands,
    Saffron bright from Spain.

Here's pepper hot from Singapore,
    Tea from an Indian hill,
Cocoa that blooms in the high Cameroons,
    Coffee from Brazil.

"Here's caraway and coriander, cardamon and sage—" he sang, "but I can see you don't need those today, so you won't get the rhymes

for them till the spice drawers are empty."
He shook his head. "Ah, the spice business
isn't what it used to be. Too many people eat
everything plain-boiled these days. You must
get your mother to use more coriander, Anna
Lavinia. I have a lovely rhyme for that, and
it came from such a wonderful place."

"Where did you find the rhyme?" she
asked.

"Why, it was in—" Her Uncle Jeffrey
stopped short and burst out laughing. "You
almost caught me there, Anna Lavinia," he
said, and he reached across the table to tweak

her ear again. "Let's just say that in wandering up and down I found a rhyme somewhere. You're getting clever, Anna Lavinia, and more like your father every day. Even your hair is just as red."

As though to change the subject, Uncle Jeffrey plunged his arm deep into his knapsack and plucked out a scuffed red leather notebook, fastened with shining silver clasps. "I suppose you will want to look at this again today," he said, sliding it across the table to her. "There are some wonderful new things in it."

Anna Lavinia's fingers fumbled with the clasps. To look at that notebook was the special treat of each of Uncle Jeffrey's visits.

Between the pages he had carefully pressed the strange flowers and leaves which he gathered on his travels. Of some he knew the names, and he had written the hard-sounding Latin words on the page. For the rest he jotted down the names of the places where he collected them.

Anna Lavinia turned the pages gently, so as not to crack the brittle leaves. She saw in turn wild mountain flowers with petals like plush, feathery cactus blossoms pressed so thin that light shone through, streaked tulips small as a thumbnail, and crisp everlastings bright as the flash of hummingbirds' wings. At last she came to a fragile purple flower with five fringed petals.

"Is this a new one?" she asked. "I haven't seen it before."

"New? No, Anna Lavinia," he answered. "It has always been there. It was the first I put in the book."

Anna Lavinia then saw that the strange flower was set off from the rest by two blank pages either side of it. For that reason she must have skipped it before.

"It has no name written down," she said, "but it looks like a rose. Is it?"

Uncle Jeffrey's eyes were bright as he answered, "The loveliest rose of all. I remember a bush that grew beside a stream, and the purple petals as they drifted would float upon the air, perfuming it as they passed."

Anna Lavinia sniffed the dry rose, but she could smell no trace of the odor. She fastened the clasps of the notebook and shoved it back across the table. "You didn't write down where it came from, though you usually do," she said.

Uncle Jeffrey chuckled and tucked the

notebook in his knapsack. "After all, Anna Lavinia," he said, "you don't expect me to remember everything, do you?"

Perhaps not, she thought, reaching for a sandwich. That first flower must have been picked years ago. Yet she could not help thinking that there was something special about it that had made Uncle Jeffrey set it off from the rest.

CHAPTER 3

TOWARDS DEW POND HILL

AFTER LUNCH Anna Lavinia's mother set her to peeling onions, while she put pawpaws on the stove to simmer. Uncle Jeffrey leaned back in his chair, humming "Over the Hills and Far Away" and puffing at a clay pipe. The pleasant smoke took away some of the onion smell, but it could not stop the tears which smarted in Anna Lavinia's eyes.

"If you peel onions under water, Anna Lavinia," her mother said, "you won't blubber so much."

"May I take them to the spring, then?" Anna Lavinia asked. Nothing could be more pleasant than to sit on a stone in the stream, with her feet tickling on the pebbles.

Her mother laughed, "Well, I didn't mean for you to be under water too—only the onions. I don't think that would work at all."

"Here," Uncle Jeffrey said. "Let me peel the onions. Nothing makes me weep. When you get to be as old as I am, you're pretty well done with tears."

Anna Lavinia wiped her eyes with the hem of her dress. "Do you mean, even if something were very sad, you couldn't cry at all?" she asked.

"Oh, I might feel it here," he answered, thumping his chest so hard that the petals flew from the pink buttercup in his buttonhole. "But my eyes would be as dry as your well. After all, sadness depends on your point of view."

"I don't think I'll ever run dry, then," Anna Lavinia said. "Not so long as my point of view has a dew pond in it." With that she slipped out onto the back stoop to have a squint at it.

One small cloud was passing overhead. She watched its shadow move across the lawn. It slipped through the hole in the garden wall and rippled over the meadow towards Dew Pond Hill. The three men with shovels were still digging, and their shovels flashed in the sun. Somehow the hole in the wall had never called, "Come!" quite so strongly before. Anna Lavinia stepped down from the stoop.

She had moved halfway across the yard when she heard her mother call, "And where are you off to now?"

Anna Lavinia stopped. "I just wanted to see what those men are digging for over by Dew Pond Hill," she said.

Her mother considered. "Well," she said finally, "I suppose your Uncle Jeffrey will get me more water when I need it. But put on your shoes and stockings. I don't want you running barefoot like a gypsy."

Anna Lavinia ran back to the kitchen. As she struggled with her shoes, she asked, "Uncle Jeffrey, don't gypsies ever wear shoes?"

"I've seen a good many gypsies," he answered, "but never a one with shoes. They like too well the feel of the road. You know the ballad of the girl who danced off with the gypsies, don't you?"

Before Anna Lavinia could answer, he began to sing:

Giddy Liddy Gandaway
Plotted late and planned away,
Sold her home and land away,
To join the gypsy jugglers
And to drive their crimson van.

Giddy Liddy Gandaway
Tripped the saraband away,
Gave her lily hand away,
To wed a turbaned tinker
With a jeweled frying pan.

Giddy Liddy Gandaway
Danced the gypsy band away,
Tambourined to Mandalay,
To cool the temple monkeys
With a silver gilded fan.

Giddy Liddy Gandaway
Faded while she fanned away,
Flew like chaff or sand away,
To vanish as completely
As the windblown winnowed bran.

As soon as the song was finished, the parrot

on the back stoop began screaming, "Giddy Liddy! Giddy Liddy! I must have biscuits too!"

"Now, see what you have done!" Anna Lavinia's mother exclaimed. "Just when I was beginning to think the parrot was going to keep quiet for good."

Anna Lavinia knew that it was a very good sign for the parrot to be talking again, even if it mixed up two songs. As she started to leave the kitchen, her Uncle Jeffrey caught her by the ear.

"What's this about a dew pond?" he demanded. "I shouldn't go near one if I were you. Dew ponds are bewitched."

"Bewitched?" Anna Lavinia asked.

Uncle Jeffrey nodded. "Sort of, anyway. Dew ponds got me into trouble once or twice. You see, wherever water—"

Interrupting him, Anna Lavinia's mother shook her wooden spoon in the air, and the pawpaw juice splattered green across the floor. "I won't have you filling her ears with rub-

bish about dew ponds now! Your foolishness about tears was enough nonsense. No more tears, indeed! Why, if I couldn't have a good cry whenever I felt like it, I don't know what I'd do. If Anna Lavinia wants to look at the dew pond, she may. Her father promised to take her there sometime, and goodness knows when he'll be here to do it."

Anna Lavinia saw that the onions were beginning to make her mother cry again, so she hurried out the door before her mother could change her mind.

In no time at all she had scrambled through the opening in the wall and was deep in the uncut meadow beyond. The noonday sky

pressed down upon the field like a blue bowl turned upside down. Grasshoppers rustled among the towering weeds as she passed through, and fieldmice fled squeaking into hidden nests.

Now and again Anna Lavinia had to stop to pluck off the burrs that stuck to her dress or caught on a stocking just where it went into a shoe. When she stopped, the silence of the meadow made her feel a thousand miles from nowhere. Then it seemed she was a ship at sea, with only the crest of Dew Pond Hill rising above the waves of asters as a landmark to guide her. Not until she moved on, parting the tall stalks to pass between, would the

cracklings to either side let her know that she was not alone. The feeling that she was being watched finally became so uncomfortable that she was glad suddenly to find herself at the end of the meadow, on the edge of a wide field of parsnips.

From where she stood, Anna Lavinia saw that the three men had been digging a number of shallow ditches which went all the way round the parsnip field and criss-crossed it like a checkerboard. Walking between the drooping parsnips, she headed towards the ditch where the men were digging. They were singing, and their shovels swung in time with their song:

Shovel to a roundelay!
Dig a hole to Mandalay.
Heave the earth until we're through.
How many miles to Timbuctoo?
   Dig! Dig!

Heap the gravel, pile the sand!
Not so far as Samarkand.
Sparkle your shovel, flashing fire.
First into Nineveh, then into Tyre.
   Dig! Dig!

Shovel to a roundelay!
Shall we ever reach Cathay?
We are digging, if you ask us,
All the way down to Damascus.
   Dig! Dig!

"If you're going all that way," Anna Lavinia asked, "wouldn't it be better to dig just in one place, and not all around the field?"

The men wiped their red faces with bright blue pocket handkerchiefs. The first man, who was very fat, smiled and answered, "We haven't really decided where to go yet, you see."

The second man, who was very thin, laughed, adding, "Haven't you heard the longest way round is the best?"

The third man, who was very short, did not smile at all, though he had a gold tooth. "Don't believe them," he said. "All we are doing is digging a ditch to run water in. We're going to drain that pond up there."

Anna Lavinia was heartbroken. Lately she had thought of the dew pond as her very own. "But why?" she asked. "Did you lose something in it?"

The men laughed. The fat one said, "We need the water for the parsnips." He pointed to a long string which ran up the hill to guide them. When they dug through the last bit of trench, he explained, all the water in the pond would rush down the hill by gravity and fill the ditches of the parsnip field.

"Then will there never be a dew pond up there any more?" Anna Lavinia asked.

"Eventually," the fat man answered. "When we have taken the water, we'll close the ditch, so the pond can fill up. Naturally, it will take some time."

"Then I'd better hurry on up, if I want to see it full," she said, hopping across the ditch.

"There's no hurry," the thin man said. "We probably won't finish soon. We never do today what we can put off till tomorrow."

As she started up the hill, the short man

called, "Did that creature come with you, or
did we dig it up?"

Anna Lavinia looked back. Running after
her was the thobby. No wonder she had felt
that she was being followed across the
meadow. "You didn't dig him up," she called
back. "He's mine."

"It's a funny sort of pet to have," the
short man remarked.

"He's nice to pet," she answered. "And I
have a cat at home, and a parrot too. And a
hedgehog, though I don't pet that."

The men laughed as they turned to their
digging, and the fat one said to the others,
"She certainly lives in a world of her own!"

Anna Lavinia did not answer, though she
knew what he said could not be true. A world
of her own? Why, even her point of view was
being dug up before she had a chance to ex-
plore it.

CHAPTER 4

ANOTHER POINT OF VIEW

CRADLED in a hollow on the top of the hill, the dew pond was ringed with a dark grove of ancient oaks. The birds that nested in the trees stayed in the highest sunny branches, and squirrels seemed never to have gathered the acorns which covered the mossy floor. Rusty ferns and strange colored mushrooms grew from the trunks of the oaks, whose branches arched over the water. Night after night for hundreds of years the dew had trickled from the leaves to keep brimful the quiet pool below.

Tired from the long climb, Anna Lavinia sat on a cushion of moss which covered a grey stone jutting out over the water. From a branch overhead a red leaf spun down and rippled the still surface. Ring within ring expanded until the water grew still. This, then, was the lovely spot—her dew pond, her point of view—which those men with their shovels were going to spoil. It was not right, Anna Lavinia thought, to ruin all this for a field of parsnips. She reached across the moss to gather a handful of acorns, and one by one she threw them into the water as hard as she could. As she flung them, she repeated a bit of the diggers' song, "All the way down to— wherever it is."

She had not thrown more than half a dozen of the acorns when something happened that

made her jump to her feet and step back from
the edge of the water. An acorn had leaped
back out of the pond, striking her out-
stretched arm and then falling to the moss at
her feet!

For half a minute Anna Lavinia stared at
the acorn. Then she laughed. Surely, if the

acorn had come from the water, it would have been wet. The acorn on the moss was perfectly dry. If it had bounced from the water, there ought to be ripples on the dew pond. There was none. It must have fallen from a branch overhead. She must have seen only the reflection of the acorn falling from above.

Yet the spot where the acorn had struck the underside of her arm still stung. Rubbing it, Anna Lavinia realized that if the acorn had fallen from above, it could not have struck that part of her arm. She looked at the acorn again. It was old and brown. An acorn newly fallen would be green.

She picked over the acorns lying about her, and she found a very fat one with a crooked cap. From the underside of the collar of her dress she took a pin and pushed it deep into the acorn. There would be no mistaking it now if she saw it again. Tiptoe on the rock, she flung the acorn into the water. It sank without a ripple.

Anna Lavinia waited. Nothing happened. A leaf sailed across the water, spreading a track of ripples. The thobby, having seen enough of the dew pond, moved towards the sunlight, crackling dry leaves as he went. Anna Lavinia was turning to follow him when the acorn appeared again.

This time there was no chance of being mistaken. The acorn shot from the water high into the air and fell at her feet. It was the same fat acorn with the crooked cap and the pin pushed through it. But this time, fastened to it with the pin, was a scrap of yellow paper, perfectly dry. Written in pencil on it, in handwriting a little like her own, but not so neat, was the message, "Please don't throw acorns at me."

Anna Lavinia knelt on the moss and looked
deep into the water. There where her own reflection should have been, she saw looking up
at her the face of a yellow-haired boy wearing a blue shirt and a long-sleeved green
sweater with two pockets and buttons down
the front. He too appeared to be leaning over
a mossy rock, and behind him the branches of
oak trees arched beneath a sky of the deepest
lavender blue.

Anna Lavinia leaned over the edge of her rock, thinking that she would find the boy hiding beneath the ledge. There was no space there for anyone to be. The boy burst out laughing. She heard his laughter faintly, as though he were in a well.

"I don't think it's polite to laugh in a person's face," she called down to him.

"I'm sorry," the boy answered, "only you looked so surprised I couldn't help it."

"Where are you, anyway?" she asked.

"The other side of the pond," he answered. "Where else?"

Anna Lavinia looked across the dew pond. No one was there.

"The underside, I mean," the boy called out, laughing again.

His remark seemed so puzzling to Anna Lavinia that she threw an acorn at him and reached down to splash away the curious reflection.

When the ripples died away, the boy was still there, rubbing his nose where the acorn struck it. "That hurt!" he said.

"This time, I'm sorry," Anna Lavinia called down. "But, really, where are you? You're not in the water?"

"Of course not," he answered. "I don't look like a fish, do I? I was just peacefully sailing a boat down here, when you started throwing acorns at me."

"I don't see any boat," she said.

Anna Lavinia saw him reach to pick something out of the water. When he touched it, the water clouded over, and it was a moment until it became clear again. Then she saw that he was holding, sideways so that she might see it, a little sailing ship with wooden masts and linen sails. By squinting she could read the name painted on the side. It was *The Golden Salamander*, and the carved figurehead was a tiny gold lizard, rather like the thobby.

"How nice!" she exclaimed. "What's your name, anyway?"

"Tobias," he answered, "but you may call me Toby. What's yours?"

Anna Lavinia told him. Then she asked, "Why don't you come up here?"

Toby looked disappointed. "I couldn't," he said. "I promised my mother that I never would."

"But could you, if she let you?" Anna Lavinia asked.

"Easily," Toby answered. "Just like the acorns. Or you could come down here if you wanted to."

"I could?" Anna Lavinia asked eagerly.

"Simply by jumping as hard as you can," Toby said. "But the water must be very still on either side. Not a ripple, or you won't get through."

"I'd get all wet!" Anna Lavinia cried.

"Not if you do it right," he said. "The acorns didn't get wet, did they?"

"And what if I didn't do it right?" she asked.

Toby smiled. "The worst that could happen would be that you'd get wet and be scolded when you got home."

"Wait just a minute," Anna Lavinia called. She ran through the trees to find the

thobby. He was sitting at the edge of the hilltop in the sun. At the foot of the hill the three men were lying asleep in the shade of a sassafras tree. All the way back to the dew pond the thobby struggled in her arms.

"I thought you weren't coming back," Toby called to her.

Anna Lavinia stood on the rock, looking down at Toby. He now sat with his feet dangling over the edge of his stone. She saw that one of his shoes had a hole in the sole.

"There's just one thing," she said. "You're not an elf or a goblin or anything like that, are you? Because I don't believe in such things."

Toby was laughing so hard that he could scarcely answer. "Of course, I'm not. Anyway, if you don't believe, why bother to ask?"

"My uncle says that dew ponds are bewitched," she explained.

"Pooh!" Toby cried. "What do grown-ups know?"

"There's something else," she said, hesitating a little. "If you are looking up at me, you must be upside down."

Toby rolled over, so that only the back of his head showed. "If you like it better, I'll turn this way," he said. "Upside down or downside up depends on your point of view."

"That's true," she said, "but you're still

48

upside down from my point of view, like a fly
on a ceiling. What about gravity?"

"I've heard of it," Toby said. "It's something you have to put up with. We don't have
any." He held his toy boat before him and
quickly drew his hands away from it.
"Look!" he cried. The boat hung in the air
exactly where he had left it.

"How wonderful that you can do that!"
Anna Lavinia exclaimed. "Do it with something else."

Toby stuck an acorn in the air before him.
He leaned towards it and blew gently. The
acorn sailed slowly out of sight.

"I hope I won't blow about like that when
I come," she said.

"That's something you don't need to worry about," Toby answered. "As soon as you get here, you'll find out why."

"You're sure you can catch me?" she asked.

Toby pointed to an oak on his side of the pond. Stretched between two of its branches was a woven net. "You're just afraid to come," he teased. "Girls are always afraid to do anything."

Anna Lavinia did not bother to answer. With the thobby held close in her arms, she took a deep breath, squeezed shut her eyes, and jumped. Passing through the air she wondered whether she should have plunged head first instead. Now it was a little late to ask.

CHAPTER 5

TOUCH OF THE TINGLE

ELL! You really made it," Toby cried, delighted. "You see, you didn't get wet at all."

Anna Lavinia was lying on her back in the hammock-like net where she had landed. Behind her, beyond the net, was the sky. Below her, on the ground, Toby stood near the water's edge at the foot of the oak in which the net was spread. Anna Lavinia smiled, and she wanted to answer Toby, but she was too much surprised at the strange way she felt to be able to speak.

From the tips of her toes to the top of her head she tingled with a wonderful new feeling, unlike anything she had known before. It was something like the touch of clean cool sheets after a bath on a hot summer night, or the smell of the first burning leaves in autumn. It was like the taste of the first wild strawberry in springtime, or the sound of a train's whistle far off at midnight in winter. It was a little, too, like the tickle before a sneeze, or the thrill that comes when the knot in the ribbon of a gift just begins to loosen. It was like all these things rolled together, only it was even better.

Anna Lavinia shut her eyes and counted three before opening them again. The tingle was still there. The thobby in her arms felt it too, for he was trembling.

"Toby," she whispered, "I feel so wonderful. What is it? I tingle."

"You like it, then?" he asked. "You never feel that way on your side of the pond?"

"Once in a blue moon, maybe," she said. "But what is it?"

"The tingle is what we have instead of gravity down here," Toby answered. "Without gravity things do drift, if they are loose in the air. But the tingle runs through all the ground. It flows into whatever touches the ground, so that whatever touches earth then tingles too. And whatever has the tingle running through it stays put, wherever it happens to be."

While he was talking, to show what he meant, Toby took an acorn and placed it on the tip of his nose, where it rested like a feather on a cat's chin. "This will stay right where it is," he said. "Until I move it, of course. For the force of the tingle isn't so strong that it keeps you from moving things or walking about. But it's a little like a magnet."

"If the earth is like a magnet here," Anna Lavinia said, "I'd think it would pull me right out of the net and down to the ground." She ran her fingers through the net to hold fast. As her fingers gripped the net she felt the tingle even more strongly.

"But the tingle of the earth is holding you right now!" Toby said. "You don't have to clutch the net. The tingle runs up from the ground through the tree trunk and out into the branches and into the net and from the net to you. You can't come loose any more than a row of pins and needles can come loose from a magnet, without being shaken. The only difference between the tingle and a magnet is that a magnet can draw things to it: things don't have to touch a magnet to be attracted. But the earth here cannot attract what does not touch it. To have the tingle run through you and hold you, you must always be touching something that is tingling. Perhaps, really, it is more like electricity."

"Just the same, I'll feel safer when I'm on the ground," Anna Lavinia said.

"Here, give me your hand," Toby said, reaching up an arm.

Anna Lavinia gripped Toby's hand in hers, and at his touch she felt a stronger tingle as he drew her lightly to earth. The moment her feet touched the ground she felt the tingle of the earth at its very strongest. She stretched out on the grass, gripping a fat clump of weeds in each hand.

Toby sat beside her, holding the thobby. "You'll get used to it in a few minutes," he said. "Remember, you're all right so long as you feel the tingle. By the way, does this animal of yours hop?"

"He can," she said.

"In that case, we'd better tie him to something," Toby said. "You wouldn't want to lose him." He took a piece of twine from his pocket, and he tied one end to a blackberry bush. The other end he began to tie around the thobby's neck.

"Not too tight," Anna Lavinia warned. "If he hopped, wouldn't the tingle hold him?"

"Not if he jumped free of it into the air," Toby said. "He'd get stuck in the air and drift like thistledown."

"Not forever, I hope," Anna Lavinia said.

"Just until the wind blew him to earth somewhere, or drifted him into a tree top," he said.

"You mean that if I skipped or jumped

now, I'd lose the tingle too, and get stuck in the air?" she asked.

"That's nothing to be afraid of," Toby said. "It happens all the time. If by accident you jump into the air, you can always wiggle your way back to earth. Look!"

He turned a cartwheel, standing on his hands. Then slowly he drew first one arm and then the other into the air, so that he hung head downwards about two feet above the ground. His body swayed a little in the breeze. Darting his hands to the ground again, Toby drew himself to his feet.

57

"I wouldn't do it on a windy day, though," he said.

"How easy it is!" Anna Lavinia exclaimed.

"It is easy," Toby said, "except for one thing: it makes you dizzy. When you are in the air you don't feel the tingle, and without that everything is queer. You feel loose in the middle."

"Then you couldn't fly, could you?" she asked.

"Not without wings," he said. "I sometimes wonder how even birds can stay in the air so long without the tingle."

"I think it's a bit dangerous down here," Anna Lavinia said. "Think what would happen if little birds hopped out of their nest by mistake."

"Well, what does happen?" Toby asked.

"They drift a bit, and then their mother flies after them and brings them back safely. On your side, if the bird falls out of the nest, look what happens to it. The advantages are all on our side. With your gravity, if you tumble out of a window, you break your head. Here, if I go out a window, I can just walk down the side of the house."

As he spoke Toby walked over to a tree and without holding on walked straight up the trunk. He turned around and walked down again smiling.

"I want to try that!" Anna Lavinia cried eagerly, getting to her feet and walking to the tree. Gingerly she took three steps up the trunk. It was quite as easy as it seemed when Toby did it, and she continued up the trunk to the first big branches, where she stopped and look around her.

Unlike her own dew pond, Toby's pond lay in a valley. On either side low hills shut out the farther view, while beyond the pond the ground grew marshy, with reeds and cat-tails growing in clumps. When the wind passed through weeping willow trees in the

distance, their thin branches streamed out-wards in the air, remaining where they were blown until the breeze tossed them another way.

Walking down the trunk again Anna La-vinia went over to the thobby to see that he was all right. Tied fast, he had burrowed himself a little cave in the moist earth, and he crouched in it with his eyes tight shut.

"You know," she said to Toby, who was

tying his boat to a stone beside the pond, "it doesn't seem at all as though I were walking on the inside of a ball."

"Why should it?" Toby asked. "When you're on the other side does it seem as though you are walking on the outside of a ball?"

"I suppose not," she answered, "though you can see that the sun is round, and the moon." She stopped. "But you can't see the sun or moon here!"

"Only through the dew pond, or other places where there is quiet water on both sides," he said. "That's why it may seem a little dim down here. All our light comes through clear water, where there are lakes and ponds on both your side and ours."

"It's cooler here, too," she said.

Toby unbuttoned his sweater and handed it to her. "Put this on," he said.

"Don't let me forget to give it back when I go," she warned. "By the way, since things can't fall here, I shouldn't think it ever rains."

"Oh, a driving rain, blown by the wind, will come to earth," he said. "And afterwards the air is filled with hanging raindrops, until they dry away."

"A good windstorm must send a lot of things drifting about," Anna Lavinia reflected.

"It does," Toby said. "But when that happens the recovery patrol goes to work. Especially over villages." He waved in the direction of the hills beyond the pond. "If your eyes are sharp, you may be able to see some of the men at work over the village now. Can you see those tall poles?"

Anna Lavinia squinted. She could just make out that there were figures moving between the poles in what seemed to be wicker baskets.

"The recovery patrol works from ropes strung between the poles," he said. "They gather whatever may have drifted—tree branches, or laundry lost from clotheslines—things like that. Just last week I lost my best penknife, whittling in the wind. But that probably won't ever be recovered.

"Patrol isn't hard work," he went on, "but it isn't pleasant. The poles are so tall and the ropes so thin that the tingle isn't very strong up there. After a few hours you get dizzy. So the duty is divided equally. My father is on it now. It has one advantage, though. Sometimes you find good things on patrol, and if no one claims them, then finders keepers. Last time my father was on patrol, he found this and gave it to me when no one claimed it."

Toby pulled from his pocket a shabby little water-stained book, very much shaken by the wind, and lacking a cover. "It's a songbook," he said, and he began to read:

> No room for me
>   To go for the ride?
> No room for me?
>   Oh, please!
>
> I'm sure there's room
>   If you only tried,
> If you only tried—
>   To squeeze!

"How strange!" Anna Lavinia cried. "I know that! It's the second piece in the book, *Songs from Nowhere.*"

CHAPTER 6

SONGS FROM NOWHERE

T CAN'T BE the same book, then," Toby
said. "The song I just read is the first
one here."

"A page must be missing, along with the
cover," Anna Lavinia said. "Turn that page
and read the next one. Then I can tell."

Toby hesitated. "Oh, no," he said. "No
matter what I read, you can say it comes next.

You tell me instead what the next page is about."

"I'll do better than that," she said. "I'll sing it." And she sang:

> Remember yesterday?
> You said it then:
> "I never want to play
> With you again!"

> Today, across the hedge,
> A different song:
> "May I play too?" Oh? Well—
> Yes! Come along.

"You're right!" Toby said. "It is the same. And down here too!"

"Come to think of it," Anna Lavinia remarked, "I lost a copy of that book once. I don't suppose it would be the same one, though." She reached for the tattered book. "Let me look at it, just for fun."

Toby held tight. "And let you thumb through to a torn page and say you remembered the tear? Oh, no! If you want to claim it, you have to identify it. That's the rule of recovery patrol."

"Silly!" Anna Lavinia said. "I don't want to claim it. I have a brand-new copy at home. I was just curious." She thought a moment. "There is a way I can tell if it was mine. Turn to the page with the picture of the two owls."

Toby shuffled the pages. "I've found it," he said.

"Now, read the lines," she said.

Toby read:

> For every owl that calls To-wit!
>   Another hoots To-woo!
> For every up there is a down,
>   For each begun a through.
>
> Each clock to tock must also tick,
>   Each whereas has a therefore,
> So there are reasons, I suppose,
>   For things I do not care for.

"Well, do you see anything funny about the page?" she asked.

"Do you mean the line, 'For every up there

is a down'? That's not true—at least not down here," Toby said.

"No, I mean something drawn there," she said. "In colored pencil. Yellow and blue."

"You win," Toby said. "There is something there, though it's nearly washed away. It looks like a yellow square and a blue mug."

"It's a riddle I drew," Anna Lavinia explained. "One of the things I do not care for. Can't you guess?"

Toby thought. "Well, the yellow could be cheese, and the mug could be water. What's wrong with cheese and water?"

"Wrong!" she said. "It's buttermilk. I hate it."

"I knew it all the time," he said. "But how could your book get down here? You didn't pitch it in the pond?"

"Never," she said. "All I remember is that it was missing one day—the day after I was punished for throwing pawpaw pits in our well."

"Do you remember the song on the page that's missing?" Toby asked.

Anna Lavinia nodded. "Maybe I'll sing it to you sometime when you visit me on the other side of the pond."

Toby shook his head. "I'm afraid I'll never hear it then. I couldn't go."

"Even if your mother finally said you might?" she asked.

"She never would let me," he said. "Mother is old-fashioned. It's only lately that anyone on this side is permitted to go over to your side and return again."

"What happened before that?" Anna Lavinia said.

"Anyone could go, naturally, whenever they wanted to. But if they came back again," he said, "they were forbidden to stay."

"They were banished?" Anna Lavinia asked. "But why?"

"Too many were nipping out when it was

their time to go on recovery patrol," he said, "or just because they were curious."

"I would have come back again anyway," Anna Lavinia said.

"Some did," Toby said, "only to be banished again. Twice removed, they usually stayed on the other side for good."

"You said it's all right to come back now, though," she said.

Toby pointed to a bright yellow printed notice tacked to one of the trees. "That's the proclamation that says so. Those who have been banished may return, and those who are here may go out. But I don't know anyone who would go up there for anything in the world."

"Why not?" Anna Lavinia protested. "There's nothing wrong with being on the other side."

"Not for you, perhaps," he said, "but for any of us it is too hard on the legs. Our legs aren't used to carrying all the weight of gravity. Those few who have come back are all bandy-legged. Anyway, I wouldn't want to be without the tingle."

"Well, there are disadvantages either way," Anna Lavinia said, "if you're not used to it. Right now my head feels a little strange."

"Better lie down on the ground for a moment," Toby said.

Stretched out on the grass Anna Lavinia felt much better. She plucked a handful of wild spearmint and threw the stalks far into the air, watching them scatter slowly in the gentle wind. Where would they drift to, in that sky which grew darker in the lavender blue distance?

"Toby," she said softly, "if, by chance, someone drifted and didn't get back, where would they go?"

"I don't know," he answered. "I don't think anybody does. There have been stories written about it, though no one actually has ever been lost. My favorite book is about a man who drifted away, shipwrecked in the air. He built himself an island of driftwood and finally sailed back to earth in a thunderstorm. But that was make-believe. Just as Aunt Cornelia used to say when I was little, 'The tingle will desert you if you don't behave.' It made me behave, though."

"Who is Aunt Cornelia?" Anna Lavinia asked.

"My aunt—my great-aunt, really," he said. "She lives with us, and——"

Anna Lavinia put a finger to her lips. "Shh!" she whispered. "Listen!"

Far off a sound, as of someone crying, came from the wooded hillside beyond the pond.

Toby shrugged his shoulders. "It's probably that gypsy baby. There's a gypsy caravan that's been in the wood about a week."

"Well, someone ought to see what is the matter with it," Anna Lavinia said. "And if you won't, I will. That's the trouble with boys. They have no heart."

Anna Lavinia started running in the direction of the sound, with Toby following two steps behind her.

CHAPTER 7

WHEN THE WIND BLOWS

HE WAY towards the hillside lay across the marsh beyond the pond. Anna Lavinia was surprised to find how quickly she could run. Her shoes scarcely sank in the marshy ground, so light were her steps. When she reached the edge of a large puddle, automatically she jumped to get across.

At once she knew that she had made a mistake. In jumping she had leaped free of the tingle and, instead of crossing over the puddle, she began to move slowly slantwise up into the air. Before she drifted beyond reach,

Toby was beneath her, and he drew her back to earth by her heels. The few moments in the air, however, had given her a taste of what it was to be without the tingle.

"You see how it feels?" Toby asked.

"Like spinning on a twisted swing or stepping on a step that isn't there," Anna Lavinia said. "I won't be doing that again!"

74

From then on she willingly followed Toby as he led the way around the edge of the puddle and crossed onto dry ground in the direction of the wood. At the foot of a cliff Toby stopped.

"Here you can jump again," he said, "if you want to save time, and can bear to be in the air for a moment." He sprang upwards, passing quickly along the side of the cliff until he caught hold of a twisted bush at the top.

Standing on the edge above her, he called back, "If you don't want to do it, you can just walk up the side. But watch the brambles."

Anna Lavinia did not hesitate, but leaped up towards the bush, caught it, and swung herself to stand at Toby's side. "If it weren't for the gypsy baby, I wouldn't have done it," she said, when she felt the tingle once more, "but something tells me that it is in trouble."

The gypsy baby now was crying so pitifully even Toby hurried as he led the way through the wood, pushing through tangles of bittersweet vine, so that the ripe berries shook loose into the still air.

At length the underbrush grew thinner, giving way to floor of golden-seeded moss. Soon they reached a small clearing in the trees, a gentle slope from which the ground dropped abruptly on one side. It was there the gypsies had been camping.

Anna Lavinia gave a cry of surprise as she saw at a glance what had happened. The gypsy caravan, a house-wagon brightly painted in red and blue and yellow, was

hitched to a spotted mule whose left hind foot was tethered to a tree by a long rope. In cropping grass the mule had drawn the caravan further and further from the tree. Finally he must have walked straight down the low cliff to get to the greener grass at the bottom. But his tether had been too short for him to reach the bottom, and with the caravan behind him he had not been able to back up. Unable to go one way or the other, the bewildered mule now stood with only his forelegs on the grass at the foot of the cliff. The rest of him, and the caravan behind him, extended almost straight up in the air, tingling to the side of the cliff.

Toby ran to the mule and untied the rope that held him. He then was able to lead the mule, with the caravan following after, safely to level ground. While he was tethering the mule again, Anna Lavinia stepped into the caravan through the open back door.

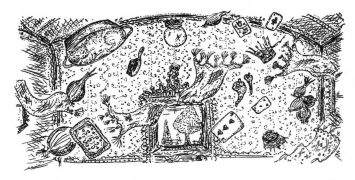

Inside everything was in disorder. Fortune-telling cards and bright silk scarves and a crystal ball, together with half-finished woven baskets and tinkering tools, red peppers and purple onions, all stuck helter-skelter to walls or ceiling, wherever the tingle held them when the caravan had jostled over the edge of the cliff. But there was not a sign of the baby.

"Do you see it?" Toby asked, entering the caravan.

"It's not here," Anna Lavinia said. "There's no one here except that grey cat, curled up in the dishpan on the ceiling."

Just then the gypsy baby broke out crying again, louder than ever. Anna Lavinia and Toby stepped down from the caravan and looked in the direction of the sound.

"There it is!" Toby cried, pointing for Anna Lavinia, who had been peering among the bushes at the edge of the clearing.

Not on the ground at all, but high in the air halfway between two beech trees, the gypsy baby floated in a wicker basket. When the caravan had passed over the cliff, the basket must have bounced loose, carrying the baby through the back door into the air. Even now, as the baby squirmed in its crying, the basket moved a few inches higher.

Anna Lavinia began running to the base of one of the beech trees, but Toby stopped her. "Where do you think you're going?"

"To climb the tree, of course, and reach out from the furthest limb and grab the basket," she said.

"Why go to all that trouble?" he asked. "We'll do this as they do it on recovery patrol."

He ran to the caravan and removed a long pole hooked to one of the sides. Standing directly beneath the baby in the basket, he tried to run the end of the pole through one of the handles of the basket. The pole was a few feet too short.

"Now what?" Anna Lavinia asked.

"I'll have to go up," Toby said. "You hold the pole tight to the ground, so the tingle is good and strong."

With one hand loosely held around the pole to guide him, Toby leaped to the very end. Even as he reached the top of the pole,

the howling baby kicked himself free of the basket. In that moment, however, Toby's fingers gripped the blue tassel of the baby's stocking cap, and he drew the baby safely to him.

"Swing us down to earth again," Toby called to Anna Lavinia.

She pushed on the pole and it swung slowly to the ground. Toby thrust the baby into her arms.

"Poor thing!" she said, holding him. "No wonder he howled so, away from the tingle."

"Can't you make him stop crying now, then?" Toby said. "Sing him a song, or bounce him on your knee."

Anna Lavinia began to sing, "Hush-a-bye, Baby," but when she came to the part, "the cradle will fall," she stopped. The baby was screaming worse than ever.

"It's no good, Toby," she said. "My kind of lullaby won't work down here. You sing something."

"I'll try the one Aunt Cornelia used to sing to me," he said, and he sang:

Now the summer-house is calling:
    Lazy daisy, drowsy fair!
Cool, the latticed shadows falling,
    Sweet, the frosty fox-grape there.

Drooped, the roses drift their petals:
    Lazy daisy, drowsy fair!
Hushed, the nesting hornet settles,
    Heavy, nods the noonday air.

Flown, the wood-dove, faint her crying:
    Lazy daisy, drowsy fair!
Closed, the morning-glories, dying,
    Thick, the silence everywhere.

Stilled, the rustlings in the willow:
    Lazy daisy, drowsy fair!
Sleep, my love, the moss your pillow,
    Dream away a world of care.

As Toby finished the lullaby, the baby smiled. At that moment the gypsy mother came running into the clearing, with a heap of mushrooms gathered into her apron. When she saw that the caravan had been moved, she threw her arms into the air, and the mushrooms began to drift like thistledown.

Seeing most of her mushrooms sliding into the air and the rest of them tingling to her clothes, the gypsy mother said one or two

words in gypsy language and rushed to the caravan, with her green skirt and purple petticoat billowing and her scarlet veil streaming.

Before she could clamber into the caravan, however, Anna Lavinia called to her from the bushes where she and Toby were sitting, half hidden. "Your baby's all right," she said. "We have him here."

84

The gypsy mother was overjoyed to find her baby safe, for she had noticed the empty basket high in the air. For five minutes she did nothing but chatter in gypsy language as she gently tossed the baby in the air and plucked him out of it again. Finally Anna Lavinia and Toby found a chance to tell her how they had rescued the baby.

"I'm sorry I couldn't reach the basket too," Toby added.

"It was getting too small for him anyway," the gypsy mother said. "Now, I want to do something for you two in return. Do you want a tin pail mended, or would you care for a little basket of cheeses made from goat's milk, or some castanets or a pair of earrings— or shall I tell you your fortunes? Come along to the van. While I put things in order, you can be deciding."

They all went to the caravan and climbed in, and it was very cosy. The gypsy mother popped the baby in a bureau drawer and shut it, all but two inches. Then she began putting

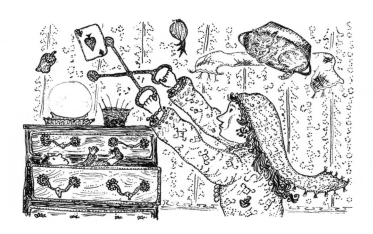

things back where they belonged, and what she could not reach with her hands she pinched down from the ceiling with a pair of fire tongs.

As his gift Toby chose a tambourine, after the gypsy mother convinced him that it was really a sort of drum. Anna Lavinia was tempted to take some round gold earrings, but she could not resist having her fortune told instead.

"It seems as though some of my fortune-telling cards must have drifted out the back door," the gypsy mother said. "I'll have to read your palm instead. So hold out your left hand."

She took Anna Lavinia's hand in hers and studied it for a long time. "It's a difficult palm to read," she said, "but here goes. Your name is Anna—"

"That's right," Anna Lavinia said encouragingly.

"Anna—let me see," the gypsy mother paused. "Anna Ainival. What a curious name!"

"That's not right," Anna Lavinia said. "My name is Anna Lavinia."

"Ainival sounds like Lavinia backwards," Toby said, shaking his tambourine at the grey cat still sleeping in the dishpan tingling to the ceiling.

"Oho! That's the trouble," cried the gypsy mother. "Your fortune is coming out backwards! You can't be from down here."

"Well, I'm not," Anna Lavinia said.

"I see," said the gypsy mother. She peered into Anna Lavinia's hand. "It looks as though an old man will make you very happy."

"That's nice," Anna Lavinia said.

"No, it's not!" the gypsy mother contradicted. "I mean, it's not right. I've got it backwards again."

Anna Lavinia was worried. "You mean an old man will make me very unhappy? I don't like that."

"No, not that either," the gypsy mother said, shutting her eyes. "Let me think a minute."

"Maybe it should be that Anna Lavinia will make an old man very happy," Toby suggested.

"That's it, exactly!" the gypsy mother cried.

"Well, it's not so bad when you put it that way," Anna Lavinia said. "What else do you see?"

"That's about all I can do today," the gypsy mother replied. "It makes me giddy to look at your hand, almost as though I'd lost the tingle. I'll tell you the rest next time I travel this way."

"You're leaving here, then?" Toby asked.

"Tomorrow morning, before the first light glitters through clear waters," she answered, wiggling the toes of her bare feet so that the brass bells on her ankles tinkled. "My feet are itching for the feel of the road."

"We've got to be going too," Toby said. "Aunt Cornelia will be wondering why I'm so long."

Anna Lavinia and Toby thanked the gypsy mother for their gifts and they left the caravan. As they walked from the clearing they could see the gypsy mother running about, scooping her scattered mushrooms out of the air with a long-handled butterfly-net, while

she sang a tinker's tune about a kettle and a
pot:

> The pot that called the kettle black
> Spied a mirror at his back.
> He blushed to see his shining metal
> Twice as tarnished as the kettle.
>
> "Forgive me, kettle!" clinked the pot,
> "I thought that I was what I'm not."
> "Forgiven, pot!" the kettle clattered,
> "Between us, do you think it mattered?"

CHAPTER 8

A TURTLE AND A
THIMBLE

I F YOU'LL SHOW me the way back to the pond, Toby," Anna Lavinia said when they left the clearing in the wood, "I think I'd better be getting home."

"Oh, not yet!" he said. "I want you to see where I live first. And have a bite to eat. Aunt Cornelia always fixes something interesting this time of day."

"But your mother might not like it," Anna Lavinia said. "If she won't let you go through to the other side, she might not approve even of the idea of your seeing me."

"I'm sure it wouldn't make any difference," Toby said. "Anyway, she's off to a net-making party in the village this afternoon. Only Aunt Cornelia will be home, and she'd be very curious to see someone from the other side."

"I don't like the way you say that," Anna Lavinia said. "As though I were a freak or something."

"Don't be silly," he said, leading the way along a path under the trees. "It's just that Aunt Cornelia has always been especially curious to know about the other side. You see, she was going to be married once, a long time ago, and the man she was to marry ran off and never came back. Aunt Cornelia has always thought he went to the other side."

"Had they quarrelled?" Anna Lavinia asked.

"Something that didn't amount to anything," Toby said. "He wanted to travel and see the world, while she wanted to settle down."

"That wasn't much to quarrel about, Anna Lavinia said. "They both were right, in their own way."

"Of course," Toby said, "and Aunt Cornelia was ready to forgive him almost right away. But it was too late. He had gone."

"That's too bad," Anna Lavinia said. "And he never came back?"

"Not that we know of," Toby said, "so Aunt Cornelia never married at all. The saddest part of the story is that just lately, since they've passed the law saying people may return, Aunt Cornelia has got the notion that her sweetheart is coming back, after all these years."

Toby went on, "Every day she gets dressed in her best clothes and sits by the fire, rocking away. And she will say, 'Today's the day that he'll be coming. I feel it in my bones.' And every night, when it's clear that he isn't coming, she'll say, 'Perhaps the winds were rippling the water on the other side, and he couldn't get through.' "

"So," he concluded, "don't let her get started talking about it, or she'll begin crying again. I hate that."

"I won't mention it," Anna Lavinia promised.

They had left the wood now, and the footpath met a white dusty road which they walked along, with the dust spreading in a cloud behind them.

"That's where I live," Toby said, pointing towards four tall pine trees.

Anna Lavinia looked. At first all she saw were the four trees planted in a square. Then she noticed that between the tree trunks there stretched a large net. It was so thickly overgrown with blue morning-glory vines that the little one-storey cottage beneath was almost hidden.

"Here you may jump as much as you

please," Toby said, as they passed beneath the net. "But we'd better go in now."

He stopped at the door to pat the head of an enormous tortoise, so old that its back was covered with moss and ferns and wild flowers which almost hid the letters JC, carved lightly within a heart on the thick shell.

"He's a practical sort of pet to have down here," Anna Lavinia said. "You can be sure he won't jump."

"He belongs to Aunt Cornelia," Toby said. "She's had him ever since she was a girl."

"What's JC for?" Anna Lavinia asked.

"Jolly Codger, Aunt Cornelia calls him," Toby replied. "The letters were on him when she first found him. But I call him Old Jungle Creeper."

"That suits him better," Anna Lavinia agreed. She paused to brush from her dress the berries and leaves which had tingled to it in the wood.

Toby showed her into the house and down a hallway towards the parlor. Anna Lavinia peeked into the bedrooms as she followed him. She thought how convenient it was to be able to stack the mops and brooms against the ceiling, with their handles sticking down within easy reach. Toby's room, she noticed, had books and clothes scattered about, sticking to the walls and ceiling, and the wallpaper was smudged with footprints.

The parlor door stood half open, and a fire burned low in the hearth. Seated in a rocking-chair by the fire was a tiny silver-haired lady, wearing an old-fashioned dress of pale pink satin. It had ivory lace cuffs and a lace collar, pinned with a gold filigree brooch set with amethysts.

"Anna Lavinia," Toby said, "this is my aunt, Miss Cornelia."

Anna Lavinia, feeling a little nervous, tried to curtsy, but it went wrong somehow. Her skirt started to drift about her knees, and she had to straighten it.

Miss Cornelia pretended not to notice. She

smiled, saying in a soft voice, "I'm so pleased to meet you. I am always happy to meet the friends Tobias brings. Do you live near here?"

Toby answered for Anna Lavinia. "She's from the other side. She came through the pond."

"Indeed!" Miss Cornelia exclaimed. "Then the water must be calm today, without much wind on either side. That is most encouraging. Tobias, slide that chair nearer to the fire for our guest. It must seem cool here to her."

Toby was moving the chair, when Miss Cornelia put a finger to her forehead and cried, "How very thoughtless of me! You probably would be more comfortable sitting on the ceiling, wouldn't you? All my life I have thought about how things must be on that upside down other side, and now when it comes to a test I slip up. Or do you say slip down?"

"We say slip up, too," Anna Lavinia answered. She did not have the heart to say that she was not used to sitting on the ceiling at home. Anyway, she thought it would be fun to try it, just to see how a fly must feel on the ceiling. So she said only, "Please don't go to any trouble for me."

"It's no trouble at all," Miss Cornelia answered. "Tobias, the step-ladder is in the hall." She turned to Anna Lavinia. "You could just tiptoe up the side of the wall, but for ladies the ladder is more dignified."

Anna Lavinia did not particularly care about being dignified, but she waited for the ladder because she felt that Miss Cornelia wanted her to. She remembered the smudged walls she had seen in Toby's bedroom. She knew Miss Cornelia would rather not run the risk of having footprints on the parlor walls.

Toby brought the step-ladder and placed the chair on the ceiling for Anna Lavinia, with its feet firmly against the white plaster. Seated there, she felt very comfortable, though the tingle was not quite so strong as on the floor.

Miss Cornelia went to the kitchen and returned with a tray bearing three dishes of
peppermint ice-cream and a platter heaped
with good things. "I'm so happy I did some
baking today," she said, raising the tray above
her head so that Anna Lavinia might serve
herself.

There were cream puffs with pink icing,
no bigger than a fingertip, and pastry cornu-
copias filled with butterscotch custard, and
heart-shaped seed-cakes prettier than valen-
tines. Anna Lavinia took as many as the edge
of her plate would hold, and then she set a
few extra in the air beside her.

"We really should have had an upside-down cake for you, Anna Lavinia," Toby joked.

"Don't talk foolishness, Tobias," Miss Cornelia said. "Remember what happened to the girl in the song who talked herself out of breath."

"I don't," Anna Lavinia said. "Would you sing it for me, please?"

Miss Cornelia set her plate in the air before her, and she began to sing:

Lucinda Prattle, foolish froth!
　　Was warned when she was young
To spare her breath to cool her broth.
　　She scoffed—and wagged her tongue.

Her birthday cake, with candles lit,
　　Stood twinkling on the table.
"Blow! Lucinda. Don't just sit!"
　　She tried—and was not able!

The candles blazed, the frosting boiled,
　　The plate grew hot to touch.
Lucinda wept. Her cake was spoiled,
　　Because—she'd talked too much!

Her windy words, Lucinda learned,
　　Were better kept in storage,
To save her cake from being burned,
　　Or cool her soup and porridge.

"I like that!" Anna Lavinia exclaimed. "Though it does seem that all foolish girls in songs have names beginning with L. Liddy and Lucinda and Lucy too. You know the Lucy one?" She sang:

Underneath the weeping willow
Lucy perched upon a pillow,
Paddling sadly with a broken paddle.

But there wasn't any water,
Four fat Fidgets came and caught her,
And they put her on a peacock with a saddle.

When the ice-cream was finished and the last cake-crumb was pinched from the air, Miss Cornelia took up some sewing, and she listened eagerly to the story of the rescue of the gypsy baby. As Toby told about the fortune-telling, Miss Cornelia looked up at Anna Lavinia on the ceiling, and she sighed.

"What a wonderful fortune for you, Anna Lavinia," she said. "To make an old man very happy! That's just the sort of fortune I should like. Do you suppose the gypsy woman would tell my fortune for me, Tobias?"

"If you paid her, she'd tell you anything you wanted," Toby answered. "But she's leaving tomorrow."

Miss Cornelia's hand trembled. As she nervously smoothed her skirt, she brushed the thimble from her lap. It drifted slantingly through the air and came to rest tingling to the ceiling.

"Would you, please?" Miss Cornelia asked Anna Lavinia.

Anna Lavinia went after the thimble, tiptoeing so as not to make marks on the ceiling. It was a gold thimble with an enameled band of pink crocuses around the edge.

"Thank you, my dear," Miss Cornelia said, as Anna Lavinia came down the ladder with the thimble. "I shouldn't want to lose it. My thimble is very precious to me."

"It's a pretty one," Anna Lavinia remarked.

"It is, isn't it?" Miss Cornelia said softly, turning it on her finger. She sighed again. "I once had another, just like it but silver, and I gave it away. I was young and foolish then, and I wanted to be like the girl in the old ballad. Alas! I was."

"What ballad?" Anna Lavinia asked. She did not notice that Toby was shaking his head.

Miss Cornelia put down her sewing and looked into the fire, as she sang sweetly:

I gave my love a lavender rose,
And a silver thimble to mend his hose,
And he kissed me farewell, and nobody knows
    Why my love has left me lonely.

I gave my love a sweet pomander,
Scented fair with coriander,
And he sailed on *The Golden Salamander*,
    Sailed off, to leave me lonely.

At the end of the song Miss Cornelia's voice broke. The coals in the fire-basket shifted, showering sparks up the chimney. By the blaze of firelight Miss Cornelia looked very sad and old.

Toby put his hand on her arm. "Not crying again, Aunt Cornelia?"

She shook her head. "Dry tears, Tobias. Only dry tears."

The word "dry" suddenly roused Anna Lavinia, who had been wondering whether her Uncle Jeffrey's rhymes for coriander might be the same as Miss Cornelia's. "Toby!" she cried. "The dew pond! I must get back right away."

CHAPTER 9

THE LAVENDER ROSE
BUSH

ISS CORNELIA called from the fireside as Anna Lavinia and Toby were going out the door of the cottage. "Mind you, no short cuts to the pond, Tobias," she said. "Remember, Anna Lavinia is not used to our ways down here. And, Anna Lavinia—"

107

Turning back Anna Lavinia saw Miss Cornelia smiling in her rocking-chair. "Yes?" Anna Lavinia said.

Miss Cornelia raised her forefinger with the crocus thimble on the tip. "Don't take too seriously the grumblings of an old woman. I'm not so foolish as I seem. Good-bye now, my dear."

Instead of answering, Anna Lavinia ran back into the parlor, and she kissed Miss Cornelia on the forehead. Then she hurried outside to join Toby.

As they raced along the path through the wood, Anna Lavinia told Toby for the first time about the three men who had been digging the trench to drain the dew pond on her side. Toby was very much upset.

"I only hope we're in time," he said.

He led the way along the narrow path until they reached the cliff at the spot to which they had leaped before. Here they looked down into the valley, from which the light was fading. Across the curved horizon distant pools and lakes, like golden lamps, glowed with filtered sunlight pouring through from Anna Lavinia's world. But the light from the pond was dim, and as they watched, it grew fainter and faded altogether.

Leaping down the cliffside they ran across the swamp towards the pond.

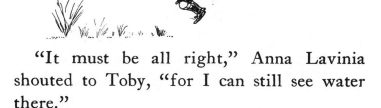

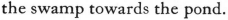

"It must be all right," Anna Lavinia shouted to Toby, "for I can still see water there."

"That doesn't mean anything," Toby said. "Draining your side of the pond wouldn't affect this side at all. The important thing is whether there is any light coming through from your side, and there isn't. No light at all."

Reaching the edge of the pond, they both looked into the water. Only their own reflections looked back at them from its surface. Beyond it was all dark.

"They've drained the other side, all right," Toby said, "and if my guess is right, the sides of the empty pond have fallen in. That's gravity for you. You can't get home that way until you've had a good rain up there. Maybe not then."

"But it hasn't rained in days," Anna Lavinia said, "and I've got to get home right now. Isn't there some other way?"

"Another dew pond, do you mean?" Toby asked. "Not that I know of. At least not for miles and miles. There are those lakes and pools we saw from the top of the cliff, but they aren't still water always. My father will know where you can get through, though. He is helping put up some patrol poles in another village now, but he'll be back in a week."

Anna Lavinia leaned against an oak tree

and blinked into the air the tears that filled
her eyes. Not to get home for a week, and
perhaps not even then! She blew impatiently
at the teardrops that hung in the air before
her nose. Who would help her mother with
the green pawpaw preserves now, or look
after the hedgehog and the parrot and Strawberry and the thobby?

The thobby! Anna Lavinia remembered
that he was here too. She rushed to look in the
little cave where she and Toby had left him
tied. The rope lay limp beside the opening.
The cave was empty.

"I should never have brought him!" she
cried. "He wriggled so, and he didn't want
to come, And now——" She looked up into the
darkening sky. "He's drifted."

"Don't start crying like the gypsy baby," Toby said. "Maybe he got back. Perhaps he got loose before the dew pond was drained."

That encouraged Anna Lavinia, and she looked about for footprints in the moist earth to make certain. Sure enough, little paw-prints of the thobby led to the edge of the pond.

"At least he made it, then," she said, "even if I can't."

"No, he didn't," Toby said slowly. "See! Here the tracks come out from the water again. He couldn't get through."

"Then we must find him quickly," she said. "If he should hop—"

"Here are some more prints," Toby said.

The tracks led towards the swamp and were hard to follow, because the thobby must have tested every puddle along the way. Luckily the marshy ground held the paw-prints very well. It was almost as though the thobby had been stamping his feet in anger. Finally the trail led out of the swamp and along a narrow stream which passed between low banks without a ripple.

"I know where we are now," Toby said. "This is the stream that leads to the sinking spring. I've been here lots of times with Aunt Cornelia."

"By sinking, do you mean it goes underground?" Anna Lavinia asked. "That's just what we want."

"I don't think it's what you want at all," he said. "You can't see light coming through where it disappears. Just because it goes under the ground doesn't prove that it comes out again on your side. Besides, for you to get through, the water must be very still on both sides. Here the water glides."

"But not very fast," Anna Lavinia remarked. "Look! Here is where the thobby went in again."

The last footprints of the thobby's hind legs were particularly deep, as though he had pushed hard to make sure that he would go down and not drift.

"He didn't come out again, anyway," Toby said.

Together they stood on the bank watching the water as it disappeared into a cave-like opening in the earth.

At last Anna Lavinia said, "Toby, I'm going to jump too."

"You can't!" he cried. "We don't know that it would work."

"I'll have to take that chance," she said. "I'll hold my breath as long as I can. But," she continued, "just in case it doesn't work, it would be best to be prepared. If you could get a piece of rope, I could tie it to something here. Then if I didn't seem to be getting through, you could pull me back."

Toby agreed to that, and he ran off in the dusk to find a rope.

While she waited Anna Lavinia looked for something to which to tie the rope. Close to the edge of the water on the other bank of the stream grew an old bush with stout spiny stems. She stepped across the stream to look at it and decided that it would do. As she stood beside the bush she caught the scent of a delicious perfume, sweeter and spicier than anything she could remember. She spread the branches apart, looking for the blossom which gave so heavenly an odor.

In the dusk as she reached to pluck the single flower, the ruffling of the leaves shook loose the petals, and they drifted in the air. Through the gloom Anna Lavinia could not be sure, but the swirling petals seemed to be lavender. She searched the whole thorny bush for another bloom, but there was none, only purple seed-pods like little rose-apples. They too smelled sweet, though not quite so pungent.

She gathered a handful and looked about
for something to wrap them in. On several
trees nearby she saw the yellow glow of the
proclamations tacked there. She felt it would
do not harm to take just one. She wrapped the
rose-apples in the paper, and she was putting
it in a sweater pocket when Toby appeared
with a rope.

"Sorry I was so long," he said. "I had to go
back to the house for the rope. I wanted to get
a new one, to be sure it would hold. Guess
what Aunt Cornelia has done!"

"Lost her thimble?" Anna Lavinia
guessed.

"No. As soon as you and I left the house,"
Toby said, "Aunt Cornelia went to the wood
to have her fortune told."

"Was it a good fortune?" Anna Lavinia asked.

"Pooh!" Toby uncoiled the rope. "The gypsy said a girl would bring Aunt Cornelia news that would make her very happy. Aunt Cornelia was disappointed. She told the gypsy mother that she had already seen the girl—meaning you—and that there was no news. It wasn't worth the bottle of her best raspberry cordial that she gave the gypsy."

"I'm sorry," Anna Lavinia said, tying one end of the rope to the old bush. "I'll try to do better for Miss Cornelia next time—if there is a next time."

She now stood at the brink of the sinking spring, at the very spot from which the thobby had jumped. There was nothing to do but go.

"Push me, Toby," she said. "Push me hard."

"I hate to do it," he said. "How will I know if you get there?"

"If it doesn't seem as though I'm getting

through," she said, "I'll tug three times on the rope. Then you must pull me back. If I do get through, and the rope is long enough, I'll jerk six times, to let you know I made it."

"Supposing the rope isn't long enough. What then?" he asked.

"Go to the dew pond tomorrow at sunrise," she said. "There should be enough dew in it on my side then for me to throw at least an acorn through, as a sign."

"One thing more, before you go," Toby said. "You never told me the song on the missing page of the book."

"But it's an all-in-one-breath song!" she protested. "I can't do it now."

"Do it anyway," he said. "It will be good practice."

"Well— Maybe it will bring good luck," she said. "But when I've finished, and taken a deep breath again, push me. Promise?"

"Promise," Toby answered, and Anna Lavinia sang the very first of the *Songs from Nowhere:*

Today I found a secret,
  Clenched it in my fist,
Tied it in a handkerchief,
  Gave each knot a twist.

Took it to my bedroom,
  Stuck it in a box,
Turned the key a dozen times,
  Jammed and plugged the locks.

Pounded flat the hinges,
  Nailed the lid with tacks,
Wrapped the box in silverfoil,
  Sealed the knots with wax.

Folded it in canvas,
  Stitched the seams up tight,
Hid it in the sugar bin,
  Waited until night.

Tiptoed in the garden,
  Dug the safest place,
Buried it beneath the grass,
  Smoothed away each trace.

Scattered leaves above it,
  Said a special spell.
Want to know what's hidden there?
  Think I'd ever tell?

When Anna Lavinia finished singing she took a deep breath, and Toby pushed her with all his strength. Holding fast to a knot on the end of the rope, she plunged into the water and disappeared in the cavity. Almost at once she knew that something was wrong, for she could feel the coldness and the wetness and the darkness of the water. Strong currents pulled her forward, and twisting counter-currents twirled her back. A sharp snap on the line, followed by a sudden slackness, let her know the rope had broken.

CHAPTER 10

WHERE STILL WATERS RUN

ER HEART was pounding, and Anna Lavinia knew she could not hold her breath a moment longer, when she felt her head bob above the water and her feet touched a stony stream bed. The tingle was gone.

Opening her eyes, she found that she was

facing a fern-covered shelf of rock from which several pairs of golden eyes blinked at her. It was a moment before she realized that they were frogs, and yet another moment before she recognized where she was.

With a laugh, she spun about in the water, which did not seem half so cold now, and she saw before her the bridge that spanned the stream on the road to the village. Toby's sinking spring was the other side of her own.

She waded from the spring and stood on one of the stepping-stones to wring out her skirt and shake the water from her ears. She noticed that she was still wearing Toby's sweater, and she took it off and hung it over the crumbling wall to dry. All the while she had the curious feeling that she was being watched, just as when she had crossed the meadow earlier in the day. This time she did not mind, for she felt that it was probably the thobby again, and she was happy that he had come through the spring safely.

It was almost dark as she climbed the em-

bankment to the road, and she ran to dry her
clothes. Again and again she jumped into the
air, because it was such a relief to know that
she would return to the ground each time.

Coming through the hole in the wall, she
crossed the lawn. As she passed the nasturtium bed she was surprised to see the thobby,

quite worn out, sound asleep in a freshly dug
hollow. It must have been Strawberry, then,
who had been spying on her at the spring, she
decided. No doubt he stayed hidden to keep
from being splashed.

A light was burning in the kitchen. Sitting
on the back stoop to take off her wet shoes,
Anna Lavinia heard her mother singing as
she set the supper table. It was a song new to
Anna Lavinia, and she listened at the door as
her mother sang:

Hold quicksilver in your hand?
Keep a castle made of sand?
Map roads to some secret land?
It never can be done.

Quicksilver seized will slip away,
Sand castles crumble in a day,
The clearest chart still leads astray,
For you, or anyone.

But find the silver, unaware,
The castle, when you did not care,
The path that ran—just anywhere,
Like magic! You have won.

"That's a pretty song, Mother," Anna Lavinia said, still standing outside the screen door, waiting to see what sort of a mood her mother was in before daring to enter with clothes dripping.

"It's all foolishness!" her mother answered. "I can't imagine what made me remember it after all these years, unless it was that I was thinking of your father. A letter came from him this afternoon. He should be home in a day or so."

At that great news Anna Lavinia knew it was safe to go into the kitchen wet. When she entered she saw Strawberry dozing under the kitchen table. So he could not have been watching her at the spring either.

"Where's Uncle Jeffrey?" Anna Lavinia asked.

"Gone," her mother answered. "He left not ten minutes ago. I wanted him to stay to supper, but he lifted the kettle lid and said he couldn't. I think he was a little angry with me for the way I scolded him at lunch about his tall tales. No tears indeed! Why, when I came back from getting the mail, your Uncle Jeffrey was talking to the parrot. As I came in the door he snuffled very suspiciously and mumbled something about the onions being strong, even for him."

Looking up from her kettle for the first time, her mother noticed Anna Lavinia's wet dress. "What ever happened to you?"

"I got a little wet in the spring," Anna Lavinia answered.

"In the spring!" her mother exclaimed. "I thought you went to the dew pond."

"I did," Anna Lavinia said.

"I suppose you were into that too?" her mother asked.

Anna Lavinia nodded.

"In one and out the other," her mother said, laughing at the very foolishness of the idea. "Well, that's like you."

"That's just the way it happened," Anna Lavinia said.

"Enough nonsense!" her mother said. "You're getting to be as bad as your Uncle Jeffrey at inventing things. Run along and get ready for supper."

Supper was mostly alphabet soup and green pawpaw preserves, and Anna Lavinia did not feel hungry. She was fishing some letters out of the soup to spell "Toby" around the edge of the plate, when her mother opened the deep drawer of the kitchen table.

"I just remembered," she said, "your Uncle Jeffrey left you a present."

"The nine sorts of catnip for Strawberry?" Anna Lavinia asked, remembering that that was the usual gift.

"No, come to think of it, he forgot all about that. It was this," her mother said, and she twirled between two fingers a little silver nutmeg.

Anna Lavinia took the nutmeg. It was hollow, and when she shook it, it rattled as though there were something inside. But she could find no way to open it.

"It's lovely," she said, admiring the filigreed designs on the shell.

"I don't think it's good for anything, though," her mother said. "Your Uncle Jeffrey said that it was a keepsake that he had carried for a long time, expecting to return it to the person who gave it to him, but he'd lost hope. So he wanted you to have it. That's your Uncle Jeffrey for you—a tall tale about nothing at all."

After supper Anna Lavinia's mother sent her to bed early, because she was afraid that she might have caught cold. Though she was tired Anna Lavinia could not sleep soundly. She kept waking up, thinking of Toby and Miss Cornelia and the gypsy mother's fortune-telling and the rose bush by the stream and the rose-apples wrapped in the proclamation still in the pocket of Toby's sweater hanging over the wall by the spring.

She had so very much wanted to ask her Uncle Jeffrey about those rose-apples, and as she lay thinking, some things he had said came into her mind. The petals had floated upon the air, perfuming it. The rose was the first flower in the collection.

Suddenly remembering something Toby had said, she sat straight up in bed. Toby said people got bowlegged when they came over from the underside. Her Uncle Jeffrey was a little bowlegged. Then he must have come from the other side originally! He was one of those who had been banished—banished twice, twice removed. And now he was gone, before she could tell him that now it was all right for him to go back.

Anna Lavinia leaped out of bed. Strawberry slept undisturbed at the foot of the coverlet. She dressed quietly. Through the window she saw the moon growing pale as the sky brightened. Opening her top bureau drawer she took out an old silver penknife with a buffalo horn handle, to replace the one Toby said he had lost whittling. Then, for good luck, she put the silver nutmeg in her pocket and tiptoed downstairs. In the kitchen she took from the jelly cupboard a jar of pawpaw jelly and a jar of the new green pawpaw preserves.

Halfway across the lawn she met the hedgehog on its way to bed beside the well. The hedgehog seemed surprised to see her and rolled over on its back. Anna Lavinia stooped to stroke its soft underside where there were no quills.

"I never knew about the underside before,"

she whispered to the hedgehog. "You see, I can pet you after all."

The hedgehog winked sleepily, and it watched Anna Lavinia as she climbed through the hole in the garden wall.

At the spring Toby's sweater lay across the mossy wall where she had left it. It was still damp when she felt in one of the pockets for the rose-apples wrapped in the proclamation. Her fingers found the rose-apples, but the yellow proclamation was gone, and the rose-apples had lost all their scent.

Anna Lavinia felt in the other pocket. She gave a cry of delight as one after another she took out nine little catnip mice all made of velvet with seed pearls for eyes, and whiskers of gold and silver thread. Each mouse was a different color of velvet, with taffeta ears to match, lined in paler satin, and each mouse

was stuffed with one of the nine sorts of catnip for the nine sorts of trouble cats get into.

Those mice were her Uncle Jeffrey's doing,
Anna Lavinia knew, and at the same time
she knew that he had found the proclamation
saying that he might return to the other side.
It must have been he who was watching her
from the bridge the night before. Why hadn't
he spoken? Did the sight of her splashing in
the spring bring unhappy memories to him?

It did not matter now, she thought, as she
planted the rose-apples along the bank of the
stream, poking them into little holes made
with a stick. The gypsy mother's fortune-telling was right after all. Anna Ainival had
helped to make an old man happy. The fortune was right backwards too, she thought,
looking at the nine mice set in a row on the
wall. An old man had made her happy also.

It seemed no use to try to get Toby's sweater
back to him through the spring, so she laid
the sweater on the grass and put the penknife
in one of the pockets. Then she rolled the jar

of pawpaw jelly and the jar of green pawpaw preserves into the sweater to weight it, and she tied it into a tight ball.

With the sweater on the end of a stick slanted across her shoulder, she hurried across the meadow towards Dew Pond Hill, which was just catching the early sunlight on its crest. Her point of view had never seemed more beautiful. Crossing the parsnip field she saw that the wilted leaves were fresh again and pearled with dew, and the ditches were brimful of water.

When she reached the top of the hill she found the dew pond empty, just as Toby had predicted. The sides, no longer held in place by the water, had in part given way, tumbling slabs of mud and fallen oak leaves across the bottom. Only in one place, just beneath the moss-covered rock from which she had jumped the day before, shimmered a small puddle of freshly fallen dew. But through it Anna Lavinia caught a glimpse of the net on the other side.

From the size of the puddle she decided to roll the sweater a little smaller. When she knelt to tie it tighter, the little silver nutmeg rolled from her pocket. It tumbled across the moss, striking with a clear tinkle the fat acorn with the crooked cap. The pin in the acorn touched a secret place on the nutmeg, and it popped open like the two halves of a peach stone, spilling out a silver thimble.

Anna Lavinia examined it. Around the edge of the thimble was an enameled border of crocuses like those on Miss Cornelia's thimble, only blue. And on the inside of the thimble, engraved within a heart, were the initials J and C, just as they had appeared on Miss Cornelia's tortoise. J for Jeffrey and C for Cornelia.

Now Anna Lavinia knew she could send to Miss Cornelia the good news which the gypsy

mother had predicted. Unwrapping the
sweater she slipped the thimble in the empty
pocket. The hollow nutmeg she would keep,
but the thimble would mean too much to
Miss Cornelia and Uncle Jeffrey for them
not to have it.

She leaned over the rock and flung the fat
acorn with the crooked cap into the puddle to
test it. A moment later she saw Toby peeping

up at her. He smiled and waved, and his lips
moved as though he were greeting her, but
the puddle was too small for any sound to
come through.

Taking careful aim, Anna Lavinia hurled
the sweater into the water. As the water
cleared, she saw that Toby had caught the
bundle. Then she waved and called good-bye,
although she knew that Toby probably could

not hear her. Even as she waved she saw the bank beneath her tremble a bit, tumbling a slab of earth over the puddle, sealing it.

The sun was well up by the time she returned home, and her mother was in the kitchen watching the tea kettle boil.

"Well, you're up early, Anna Lavinia," she said, taking the tea towel off the parrot's cage. "I was about to rap on the ceiling for you."

"I took a little early morning walk," Anna Lavinia said, and she stuck her finger in the door of the parrot's cage to tickle its bill.

The parrot winked at her, and at once it began to sing:

> My love gave me a lavender rose,
> And a silver thimble to mend my hose,
> Yet I kissed her farewell, and nobody knows
> Why I left my love so lonely.

"Where on earth did the parrot learn that!" Anna Lavinia's mother exclaimed.

"Uncle Jeffrey must have taught it," Anna Lavinia answered.

"So that's what he was doing when I went to fetch the mail," her mother said. "Silly old man, singing love songs to a parrot! What he ought to do is get married and settle down."

"That shouldn't be long," Anna Lavinia said. She reached in her pocket to touch the nutmeg keepsake. "Mother," she asked, "will you answer me a question, to prove something?"

"If it is sensible," her mother said.

"Promise?" Anna Lavinia said.

Her mother nodded.

"Well," Anna Lavinia went on, "remember, about a year ago, when you punished me for dropping pawpaw pits in the well?"

"Of course, I do," her mother said, smiling. "You were made to stay in the cupboard with the brooms. And you proceeded to sing those tiresome *Songs from Nowhere* over and over again, until I just had to let you out."

"That's what the question is about," Anna Lavinia said. "You remember, the next day I couldn't find the songbook anywhere?"

Her mother looked embarrassed. "Well,

what possible difference can it make today? You have a new copy of the book now."

"You promised to answer," Anna Lavinia reminded her mother.

"All right, then. What is the question?" Her mother waited.

Anna Lavinia asked it. "Did you throw the *Songs from Nowhere* in the spring?"

"Yes! Just as hard as I could!" her mother confessed. She came over to Anna Lavinia and kissed her. "I'm sorry, dear. I shouldn't have let myself get so angry."

"But I'm glad!" Anna Lavinia cried with pleasure. "Because that finally proves it!"

"Proves what?" her mother asked.

"That still waters aren't the only ones that sometimes run deep!" Anna Lavinia exclaimed, now guessing that the way her Uncle Jeffrey had returned was through the spring. Drenched, perhaps, but he had made it, she was sure. Without a rope to hold him, maybe he had even made it dry. How was it her mother's song went? "—Quicksilver seized will slip away."

Her mother looked at her. "Too deep for me," she said. "I'm sure I don't understand you sometimes, Anna Lavinia. Do you have any more questions?"

"Just one," she said. "Can you guess the rhyme for coriander?"

Her mother scratched her head with the handle of a wooden spoon. "That's a hard one, dear," she said, "and my mind isn't too clear just now. I suddenly have that feeling that someone is coming, and this time I know it will be your father at last. But—coriander," she repeated slowly. "Well—what about story-ender?"

"I know two better ones," Anna Lavinia said. As she sang new words of her own to an old song, the parrot joined her in the rhymes:

He made his love a sweet pomander,
Scented fair with coriander,
Home he sailed on *The Golden Salamander*,
To his love, no longer lonely.

PALMER BROWN was born in Chicago and attended Swarthmore and the University of Pennsylvania. He is the author and illustrator of five books for children, including *Beyond the Pawpaw Trees* and its sequel, *The Silver Nutmeg*; *Cheerful*; and *Hickory*. About *Beyond the Pawpaw Trees*, his first published book, Brown said: "If it has any moral at all, it is hoped that it will always be a deep secret between the author and those of his readers who still know that believing is seeing."

TITLES IN
THE NEW YORK REVIEW CHILDREN'S COLLECTION

ESTHER AVERILL
Captains of the City Streets
The Hotel Cat
Jenny and the Cat Club
Jenny Goes to Sea
Jenny's Birthday Book
Jenny's Moonlight Adventure
The School for Cats

JAMES CLOYD BOWMAN
Pecos Bill: The Greatest Cowboy of All Time

PALMER BROWN
Beyond the Pawpaw Trees
Something for Christmas

SHEILA BURNFORD
Bel Ria: Dog of War

DINO BUZZATI
The Bears' Famous Invasion of Sicily

INGRI and EDGAR PARIN D'AULAIRE
D'Aulaires' Book of Animals
D'Aulaires' Book of Norse Myths
D'Aulaires' Book of Trolls
Foxie: The Singing Dog
The Terrible Troll-Bird
Too Big
The Two Cars

EILÍS DILLON
The Island of Horses
The Lost Island

DANIEL PINKWATER
Lizard Music

ALASTAIR REID and BOB GILL
Supposing...

ALASTAIR REID and BEN SHAHN
Ounce Dice Trice

BARBARA SLEIGH
Carbonel and Calidor
Carbonel: The King of the Cats
The Kingdom of Carbonel

E. C. SPYKMAN
Terrible, Horrible Edie

FRANK TASHLIN
The Bear That Wasn't

JAMES THURBER
The 13 Clocks
The Wonderful O

ALISON UTTLEY
A Traveller in Time

T. H. WHITE
Mistress Masham's Repose

MARJORIE WINSLOW and ERIK BLEGVAD
Mud Pies and Other Recipes

REINER ZIMNIK
The Bear and the People